This Topsy and Tim
book belongs to

_____

Topsy + Tim

go on an aeroplane

Jean and Gareth Adamson

Ladybird

Published by Ladybird Books Ltd
27 Wrights Lane London W8 5TZ
A Penguin Company

5 7 9 10 8 6

© Jean and Gareth Adamson MCMXCV
This edition MCMXCVIII

Printed in Italy

Topsy and Tim were off on their
summer holidays. They were going
in an aeroplane.

The airport was very big.
Topsy and Tim had a long ride in a bus
to reach the terminal building.

Then they had a long ride on an escalator to get to the right part of the building.

Their luggage went for
a long ride too, on a
moving platform.

Topsy and Tim watched an aeroplane land.
It looked much bigger when it was
not in the sky.

The door was high off the ground.
'How will the people get out?'
asked Topsy.

'Through a special tunnel,'
said Mummy. 'You will see when
it's our turn to get on the plane.'

The loudspeaker voice announced
that Topsy and Tim's aeroplane
was ready. Soon they were walking along
a telescopic tunnel and stepping
into the aeroplane. It looked like
a very long bus.

'Welcome aboard,' said the stewardess
to Topsy and Tim.

The stewardess helped Topsy and Tim
fasten their safety belts.
She gave them some comics
and some sweets.

'Suck a sweet when the aeroplane
starts to fly,' she said. 'It will
stop your ears hurting.
Tim took two sweets.
'One for each ear,' he said.
The stewardess laughed.
'They go in your mouth,
not your ears!' she said.

The big aeroplane flew up into the sky.
Topsy and Tim watched trees and houses
grow as small as toys.
'My ears have gone funny,' said Topsy.
'You didn't suck your sweet, that's why,'
said Tim.

Topsy and Tim were flying above the clouds.
'Isn't this exciting!' said Mummy.
But the clouds went on for miles and miles.
Topsy and Tim began to fidget.

Lunch came in interesting plastic trays.
Each piece of food had its own
shaped space, like the pieces
of a jigsaw puzzle. Topsy and Tim
tried to swop pieces. The stewardess
had to clear up the mess.
Then she said, 'Topsy and Tim,
the pilot would like to talk to you.'

The stewardess took Topsy and Tim
to the pilot's cabin.
'Hello twins,' said the pilot.
'I've been hearing about you.'
He showed Topsy and Tim all the
switches and levers and dials
he used to fly the aeroplane.
'Do you think you could fly
my aeroplane?' asked the pilot.
Topsy and Tim were not sure.

They went back to their seats and
fastened their safety belts once more.
Then they pretended to be pilots.
'Will you land our aeroplane now,
please, pilots?' asked the stewardess.

Topsy and Tim could see the flaps
moving in the aeroplane's wings
to make it fly lower.
'I'm doing that when I move this lever,'
said Tim. But Topsy and Tim both knew
the real pilot was doing it.

Topsy and Tim's aeroplane landed
with hardly a bump.

'Goodbye everybody,' said Topsy and Tim. They waved goodbye to the stewardess and to the pilot up in the aeroplane's nose. Then they went to meet their luggage on another moving platform.

And that is how Topsy and Tim
flew in an aeroplane.